SOUTHPAW

Kyle Toucher

BLACK HARE PRESS SHORT READS

WARDENCLYFFE by GREGG CUNNINGHAM

HADES 11 by PAUL WARMERDAM

BLOOD AND SILK by ZOEY XOLTON

AS ABOVE, SO BENEATH by JOSHUA D. TAYLOR

THE RISE OF THE GREAT OLD ONE by JASMINE JARVIS

CHRYSALIS by KIMBERLY REI

MOUNT TERROR by E.L. GILES

THE RECKONING by STEPHANIE SCISSOM

THE SPIRIT OF RODEO by BETH W. PATTERSON

CARPE DETRITUS by TIM MENDEES

THE BOOKWORM by L.T. EMERY & ANDREAS HORT

THE SALAMANDRION by MIKE ADAMSON

THIS HIDEOUS JOY by JONATHAN INBODY

THE CORONER by J. MOTOKI

FINGERPRINT FORENSICS SHORT READS

DEAD MAN WALKING by DAVID GREEN

MR HANGMAN by SCOTT MCGREGOR

HELL HARE HOUSE SHORT READS

SEEING by PATRICK WINTERS

RAINMAKER by BILL HUGHES

TESATO'S CODE by KAREN BAYLY

THE PUB AT CROKERS CROSSING by KRIS ASHTON

THE DEVIL AND THE LOCH ARD GORGE by LEANBH PEARSON

SANCTUARY by MICHAEL J. STIEHL

JUST DESSERTS by NJ GALLEGOS

SOMETHING IN MY EYE by TERRI HAMILL

CLOWN DIARY – APPENDIX 7 by JOE OPPENHEIMER

THE YELLOWS by TOM GAMMARINO

A GREAT AND SHIFTING SEA by JOHN LEAHY

SOUTHPAW by KYLE TOUCHER

INVITED by NICOLE LITTLE

Contents

~ONE~

*S*he's been fucking.

Gideon watched the pregnant woman through the windshield of his Honda minivan. Early thirties, new running shoes, smartphone strapped to her upper arm. Bluetooth earbuds roasted the meat beneath her blonde mane. He sneered at her swollen belly, protruding like the distended gut of a starving Ethiopian kid in those old late-night commercials. *Pennies a day can save lives. Won't you please give?* World Vision, Hunger Scope, or some such guilt operation.

Oh, but she's spent time on her back. Gideon knew. *If corrupted, she could very well tilt the balance of the world in evil's favor, all by the fruit of her womb.*

He browsed the decades of gawking faces he'd collected at Tabernacle, servile with acceptance, insolent with bewilderment. Whether confronted with Sawzall or sledge, hatchet or hammer, those fallen coward's eyes never ceased to incense him. *Please don't hurt me. I know*

I am about to die, but, dear God, how can this possibly *be happening to* me?

Despite a veil of gaudy arrogance, a peacock's plume of left-handed freakishness, the brittle nature of the facade was always revealed in the end. What jellyfish they became when lashed to the pillar, character told through the crucible of suffering, mewling in the presence of Tabernacle. Drowned in motor oil. Encased in plastic and left to broil in the Mojave sun. Decapitated by a rope tied to a falling cinder block. Sewn in tandem for posterity.

In the old neighborhood in Walpurgis County, summer of 1982, Gideon's Mission took flight. The mailman, a pot-bellied fool named Lester Cornwall, executed while sipping from his thermos and thumbing through an issue of *National Geographic* intended for a stranger's mailbox.

Cornwall was a common sight in Danielsburg. After his shift, but still in uniform, he often drove the mail truck around town as his own personal vehicle. He had two habits: filling up at the local watering hole on Bleary Street and yukking it up with the cashier girls at the Food Giant. His favorite cashier was Marlee Faynor, "a single girl in trouble trying to get by," as Mother had said about her several times. Marlee often endured Cornwall's bug-eyed, sweaty-necked leering, off-color comments, and inclination toward a little checkout aisle pocket pool. On more than one occasion, an adolescent Gideon had watched him load his basket with whiskey and girlie mags, then purposely wait in Marlee's longer line—when the Express lane would have served him better.

Once Marlee's pregnancy began to show through her Food Giant smock, her face a flushed moon pie from the weight gain and ten-hour shifts on her feet, Cornwall made his move. Standing in line at an adjacent aisle, Gideon and his mother watched as Cornwall leaned over the conveyor belt, stroked Marlee's left hand with his, and murmured some obscene seduction into her ear. The girl recoiled like she'd discovered a snake in her pocket.

"Undeniable, Giddy," Mother whispered. Her hands gripped her son's shoulder and squeezed. "He is one of *them.*"

At that moment, Gideon knew. The time of his calling had come, just like his father before him. What needed to be done would be done.

In early August, a week after Marlee's very public rebuke of Cornwall's overt gesture, Gideon, barely twelve, hopped on his bicycle and, for the fifth day in a row, followed Cornwall's mail truck to Gethsemane Lane. Cornwall parked on the shoulder in the shade of a massive sycamore, and Gideon waited for an hour in the bushes and ivy, watching Cornwall feed his face; feet on the dash, pith helmet cocked jauntily to the side.

Father's voice spoke, clear and rich with his wisdom

and authority. It was as if he was standing next to the boy, mentoring—but that was impossible. Father was far away and would remain so for the rest of his days, and yet, his voice rang present and true.

Now, Gideon. This is your moment of valor. Remember, you are in the open; get in, do the job, get out.

With Cornwall's attention on the magazine, Gideon slipped from cover and approached the mail truck from behind. Heart pounding, blood pushing against the back of his eyes, he caught a glimpse of his face in Cornwall's rearview mirror—strained and nervous yet governed by focus and guile. Gideon slid the truck's door open, and Cornwall, startled with his ridiculous pith helmet and stolen magazine, dribbled coffee onto his gut. He met Gideon's gaze with that old catcher's mitt of a face, neck slick and glistening.

Gideon read the mailman's eyes: *I know you see me, boy, but the others cannot. Get along before I tell them where you live.*

"What is it, punk?" Cornwall finally spat.

Gideon offered only a long exhale in return, then jabbed Mother's garden shears into the mailman's flabby neck meat. That expression Gideon had come to know and despise, the nexus of incredulity and capitulation, bound Lester Cornwall's face like shrink-wrap. Cornwall died choking on screams—blood bubbling into foam, thermos emptying like a waterfall.

The boy got to work. Father's old Craftsman handsaw would have served better that day with a new blade, but perseverance meant a job completed. The chore was clumsy, but triumphantly exhilarating. He dropped the tools and his trophies into a big bag his sister Amy had brought home from the Food Giant.

Amy was family—not a sinister bone in her body. Gideon had his suspicions about her left-handed friend Felicia, though. He'd begun an entire notebook on Felicia, and several removal scenarios had already been drawn up. Now that he had completed his first Mission, perhaps he'd accomplish his sophomore effort before school started up in the fall. The world would not miss one less southpaw.

No time to get lost in daydreams of Felicia. Gideon rolled the bag shut, hands blood-sticky, sweet sweat streaming in the summer swelter. Cornwall's government issue pith helmet had landed on the stick shift in the same idiot angle he'd worn upon his pate. The *National Geographic* on the truck's floorboards showed a whale shark now spattered in official United States Postal Service Scarlet.

Get in, do the job, get out. Just the way Father handles things—or did *handle things.*

He was lucky there were no witnesses.

Decades later and a permanent Los Angeles

resident—yet nearly invisible in a city of eleven million—Gideon possessed a scorecard unlike any before him. With Father gone, fresh accolades may never come, but the nobility of the Mission was its own reward.

How many charms I've made from witch parts. How many talismans I've sewn and stitched. A finger for a fortune, a fortune for their fealty. How many aprons I've ruined, numberless cases of Clorox I've poured down bloody drains. I was born upon the surgeon's table, already butchered and maimed, scarred and ready for War, yet they still stare at me like a cripple with a tin cup.

Gideon looked to his lap, where his left arm terminated in a nub of scar and blunted bone. He had been taught his stump was a gift—an ugly, yet magnificent, treasure. And now, decades after dispatching Lester Cornwall, experienced and fearless, he patrolled the LA basin in his unremarkable Honda. He remained not only dedicated to a crusade embarked upon at the dawn of puberty, but more enamored than ever of his disfigurement.

It is not a deformity, Mother said in his poorly-lit memories, her dusty records crackling through the speaker in the living room. Patti Page. Jo Stafford. Love songs filled with devotion and longing when new, now relics sung by ghosts. *My Giddy, you are a special boy—born with your battle scars. What you have is a gift, a precious allowance so rarely given to us in this life. Father and I will show you how to use it and what it means. Our family has a mission, and it is the Sinistra. All of them sisters, brothers, members of the pungent underworld. The Witches of the Left Hand.*

Gideon watched the pregnant woman browse a few sidewalk vendors, admiring the necklaces and other little crafty things. Finally, she dropped into a folding chair at the Gypsy Rose Sea flower stand. With the grace of a magician, the flower stand's proprietor, a balding, rat-faced fop in a flamingo-pink blazer, drew a rose from his lapel and handed it to the woman—with his left hand, a dead giveaway.

He'd known for years that the Medusa Cult breeding program had been gathering steam here in the Southwest, and the Sinistra operatives were nearly everywhere—if you knew where and *how* to look. The Sinistra possessed their own secret sign language, a type of semaphore given to them by their Medusa Cult masters. Though considered clandestine and impenetrable by the Sinistra, Gideon had cracked the cipher, and now it served as a beacon to the enlightened, the select that *understood.*

The Flamingo Man performed chivalry's bow—left arm swept wide with the right pinned behind his back, left leg outstretched and perched on the heel of his wingtip. She enjoyed the attention, smiling wide, earbuds temporarily forgotten. After dipping her face into the rose petals, she showered him in appreciation with a melodramatic vaudeville swoon.

She offered her left hand, and Flamingo Man kissed it.

Gideon's suspicions that the pregnant woman was under the influence of Flamingo Man began to take shape. If tainted, an irredeemable blackness stirred in her belly. Membranous and vile, the hybrids breathed their mother's water, gurgling in that bloodsoup until summoned on the ninth month.

Nine is of significant numeric value. Completion.

The blonde woman's glee upon receipt of Flamingo Man's affections were not faked; but there was an innocence about her expression that gave Gideon pause.

Willing breeders were different. They were unkempt, reckless. Vacant in the eyes. Users of drugs. A lot of them now resided in Tabernacle.

Many arrows align, but she requires further study. It's possible she's only a prospect, although I'm always suspicious of what grows in a southpaw's belly. She could be nurturing a Wire-Witch, a Soulhunter, or worse: something Shadowless. In a month it will be easier for me to know; determine if its wings have sprouted.

Until then, she is without shame.

But Flamingo Man is different.

He's Sinistra.

Connected.

Gideon made his decision. Follow the man in the pink blazer, learn his routines, know his haunts, indulgences, and proclivities. Once interrogated, Flamingo Man would surrender the other cultists, and when Gideon found the co-conspirators, he'd clean house.

Upon clearing the Medusa Cult nest, sensational headlines were sure to accompany the slaughter, as the news so loves its blood. Had Gideon a team of like-minded souls, oh the grisly fame they'd manifest. But it paid to stay low, anonymous. Remain in filthy cars, shithole apartments, and thrift store clothes. Minimal bank activity. No mobile phone. No social media accounts, no email. A rotating series of disguises, especially in sparsely populated areas. No large venues. No sports, concerts, horse races, casinos, or bars. The mission consumed every waking hour of every day. The shipping container buried outside Hesperia was Tabernacle, his alone, and his newly converted disciples never missed a sermon.

After pleasantries and a small purchase, she wandered away. Gideon burned her likeness into his mind's eye. If his suspicions bore fruit, a night of reckoning for her and that winged, wiggling womb tumor awaited in the silent desert. If truly innocent, she would be exorcised, purified, and set free.

Flamingo Man, for now, had his full attention.

Kyle Toucher

22

~TWO~

It was just past sunset when Flamingo Man closed the hatch, shutting his flower stand down for the night. After he turned the keys in the padlocks with his left hand, Gideon watched him saunter across Ambrose Avenue, chin up, green scarf fluttering about his neck, hands crammed into the pockets of his pink blazer.

Arrogant fop, Gideon thought as Flamingo Man unlocked his black Citroen DS. *Even his automobile is a cruel joke; the Shark, they used to call those old Citroens. They throw it in our faces, how they stalk the hopeless, then devour them from below.*

Once the sad-eyed fish was hooked, dazzled by flamboyance and charm, eased by wit, soothed by calm voices and music, the Sinistra made their move: *Do you feel alone in this world? Haven't you noticed how unfair it all is, how you've been lied to? I know an organization that can liberate you from all of that. They'll free your mind; you'll be part of the team. Find your tribe with us, and we will repopulate the world.*

As the years brought Gideon wisdom, he realized Medusa Cult symbolism had been woven into advertising, currency, and even the facial tics of a television newsreader. Murmurs of their beliefs and whispers of their agenda wormed through electronic music, mobile phone ringtones, and the calls of carrion birds. Hollywood was a notorious hive of their activity; films were stained with their corrupt message, one of the reasons Gideon had chosen Los Angeles after leaving Walpurgis County. On his way west, Gideon had seen their bloody history rendered in the stained glass windows of churches that showed the truth on the outside—but lied to everyone inside.

But Sinistra could be neutered at the wrist.

Gideon followed Flamingo Man's black Citroen at an unobtrusive distance.

Flamingo Man lived in a hip bohemian duplex in Los Feliz, surrounded by coffee houses, trendy dive bars, and vegan restaurants big on sustainable this and that. Murals covered most of the thirties-era buildings, consisting of poorly painted civil rights heroes, cartoon electric guitars with quarter notes tumbling from their headstocks, and clueless political slogans.

Exactly the cover Sinistra minions love. They undermine idealistic, soft-brained do-gooders who've never endured anything more inconvenient than a broken air conditioner. They tell them the world is broken, and the only way to fix it is to replace humanity with their superior bloodline. They'll breed the terror from the world, they're told. This is where cancer must be excised before spawning roots and turning malignant.

Flamingo Man locked his Citroen, then bounced up the stairs. After pulling his mail and thumbing through the stack, he adjusted the address plaque hanging from a wire next to the door.

16.

Gideon's eyebrows raised. For a moment his irises were little brown dots swimming in a vast white sea of sclera.

I've run that number many times.

L=3, E=5, F=6, T=2. Left = 16. Sinister = 47. 4+7 is 11. 1+1 is 2. 16/2 is 8. 8x2 is 16. 47+16=63. 6+3=9.

9=Completion. The end of a cycle. The terminus of one Mission before the ascent of another. There's no doubt; the numbers do not lie.

My stump is a war wound, preparation for times such as these.

Flamingo Man's home was surveilled until he retired at nine o'clock. Gideon had watched him prepare his dinner in an over-sized USNS *Mercy* sweatshirt, flip channels on his flat screen. Of note was the phone call

Flamingo Man made at 7:11, which lasted four minutes and seven seconds.

7+1+1 = 9. Yes, makes sense.

4 minutes plus 7 seconds is 47. 47 = Sinister.

He's communicating with the network.

Undeniable, Giddy. Mother's voice. *He is one of* them.

Gideon scrawled his observations in a notebook, some of it in English, some of it in a proprietary numeric code, accompanied by a crude drawing of Flamingo Man's decapitated head cradled in the leaking spider of his severed hand. A plan had been drawn up, the results visualized. If Gideon had learned anything from the late-night real estate infomercials of the nineties, it was that you had to keep your goal in mind all the way to the finish line. *Positive thinking equals positive cash flow,* they'd said.

He turned left onto Hyperion Avenue, caught the I-5, and was gone.

After a meal of Campbell's soup and Diet Pepsi in his empty apartment, Gideon smoothed bag balm over the nub of his stump. Mother had done this for him at the Old House, back when the family lived in Danielsburg, not long before Father's Act of Purification set Walpurgis County alight with rumor and gossip.

Father's bloody requiem, performed in 1980 upon the steps of the Vanderbaum house, the House on Beltane

Road as it was known, may have landed the man in state prison, but the culling, by any measurement, sent a stern statement of opposition to the Medusa Cult. Cultists and their Sinistra servants, grovelers to The Architect of Zero, the adjudicator of ultimate chaos and ruin, had been dispatched in sanguine glory. The papers, operated by cultists, called Father deranged, psychotic, even evil—but Father was well aware that he'd been chosen to suffer not only debasement at the hands of lesser men but also persecution and isolation. Prison was a small price to pay for the execution of an incorruptible duty.

The proprietary cipher he'd taught his son served as their encrypted communication method— invaluable during incarceration—allowing Gideon to provide Father updates of his work in the prosecution of the Sinistra War. Gideon had been a follower of footsteps, an apprentice that surpassed his mentor. He'd done his father proud, and until his emphysema-hastened death in the prison hospital in 2014, Father rarely missed an opportunity for praise and encouragement.

Father's final note read:

Gideon,

You are the true sword-bearer, far more than a namesake of the conqueror of the Midianites. Aud the Deceiver Priest, through witchery, bade the sun to shine at midnight, and we have never forgiven the transgression. Aud toiled over books and charms, spells and secrets, ears caressed by whispers born from the lips of giants. But Aud's Sinister hand was taken. His head remains nailed to the floor of his tomb.

And lo, even as my lungs turn to paper and the very air is laborious to breathe, this Mission moves forward. We endured persecution and revilement through centuries of war, but how gloriously the authority to Harvest has passed from me to you.

Spared your cursed left hand in the womb, you were born maimed for times such as these. Whether scrawled in ancient sands or praised in song before roaring fires, your name remains upon the lips of those that seek the end of the Medusa Cult.

Knighted Gideon, Man of Valor, you have exceeded speculation and expectation. Your father roars proudly in his cage, your mother sweet with tears as she listens to her melancholy records. Our family name is forever cherished in shrines reserved for the very few. I am not one to wish for impossible things, but my desire to visit Tabernacle, bear witness to your Sermon, and stand among the faces of villains as they hear the ultimate truth, is irrefutable.

I remain imprisoned so that you remain free.

Cut them.

Cut them all.

Dawn still an hour away, Gideon sat in his Honda, watching Flamingo Man's duplex. He'd slept four and a half hours, then brought Father's velvet-wrapped letter out of his strongbox, brushed his teeth, and driven back to Los Feliz. He read it aloud repeatedly as he kept one eye on the bedroom window, waiting for Flamingo Man to flip the light and start his day.

Justice stirred primal, unrelenting as breathing. Flamingo Man's left-handed ways, and his night contact with the Sinistra network was cause for indictment. Should prosecution prove compulsory, the wretch must ultimately stand at Tabernacle—where truth is majesty, and the saw renders all men equal.

I'll watch for seven days. Take notes. Flamingo Man's interrogation will be swift and fruitful. They always confess at the foot of the pillar, when they look into the eyes of my disciples, when Mother's sad music plays.

~THREE~

A week later to the hour, a moonless sky sequestered Gideon's minivan on a ribbon of open desert road. The lane lines slipped under the headlights, little fish eager to be devoured. Neglected folds of terrain lay peppered with ruined houses and junked cars, while in the feral reaches of twisted dirt trails, lovers fought, and meth labs toiled. The night dogs prowled, and the owls saw everything.

Gideon drove east on Pearblossom Highway, collar sweaty, one gloved hand on the wheel. Lawrence Hagstrom, the Flamingo Man, lay in the back, duct-taped like a kilo of contraband. Gideon snatched Hagstrom as he swished out of a local dive bar called Fill Us Driller, juiced up on Manhattans and stupid on pills. Addiction ran like wildfire through the Sinistra ranks. One of the reasons, Gideon knew, they never saw him coming.

"But you see me now, don't you?" Gideon said over the wheezing four-banger. He glanced into the rearview, where an azure worm of tarpaulin writhed. "What is the Medusa Cult *breeding*, Flamingo Man? Will you be there when she sprouts, when the womb-cricket in that blonde woman slithers out and infects everything with its filth?"

The fog in Hagstrom's mind lifted, and the sudden memory of an object striking him from behind finally snapped him awake. He hadn't suffered a blow like that in decades; it was like being hit with a pipe wrench. He was close—Gideon used an extra-large crescent from Father's toolbox. Craftsman, of course.

"I don't know what you're talking about," Hagstrom gasped, aching for air. A ring of duct tape bundled the tarp around his head like the hood of a man headed to the gallows. Every inhalation forced the plastic to conform to the shape of his mouth. "You have me...confused with someone else."

Gideon scoffed.

"Don't lie to *me*, Southpaw."

"Please, I don't have any money, I don't know—"

"Oh, you know. Likely began with witch-board when you were young, shuffling the planchette around by your sinister little hand, giggling with the slumber party girls—"

(Not long after I ended that slovenly mailman, my sister had a slumber party. Even with Father in prison, some girls still came. I was nervous and sweating, but I

finally knifed Felicia. I only broke the skin, but still, I cut her. She cried, she bled, and Amy tried not to laugh. Felicia took her witchery elsewhere, and we never saw her again.)

"—and everyone knew you were a little bedwetter sissyboy. Did your grade school teachers attempt to correct your penmanship? They realized you couldn't be forced to become right-handed like normal people—that's how it starts—and eventually the recruited become the recruiters."

Hagstrom moaned. He'd experienced intensity in his Navy years most could not imagine, but the thought of one day being kidnapped had never crossed his mind.

"*Sixteen.* Do you think numbers can *hide* you? *Protect* you? Phone calls at seven-eleven? Your seedy dive bar *crawls* with familiars, I just know it. What are their names? How often have you fornicated with Soulhunters? Have you kissed the feet of a Wire-Witch? Signed her book? If you answer before the saw finds you, you'll dodge some awful post-amputation misery."

Post-amputation—*that* seized Hagstrom's heart. He'd been black-bagged by a violent psychotic, and God only knew how far they'd driven before he came to taped and wrapped. They could be anywhere. Fillmore. Long Beach. Bakersfield. Palmdale. He was suddenly living all the stories he'd heard about Mexico City or Mosul—easy to disappear and never be seen again.

If he mewled again, it would only reinforce the diatribe he'd endured, so, "I just sell flowers, mister," was all Hagstrom could think to say.

Gideon drove the rest of the way in silence.

~FOUR~

lamingo Man slid down the aluminum ladder like mishandled freight and hit the plywood floor with a thud. Ribbons of pain strangled his shoulders and knees. Gideon stood over him in the cool underground air.

Hagstrom could hear his captor's steady, deep breathing. Somewhere a fan turned. Speakers hummed, evidence of a stereo left unattended.

"I had this shipping container buried in 1999," Gideon said. "The man who executed the contract was also the first one executed at Tabernacle. Funny how words align. When he showed up and rolled that left-handed Bobcat backhoe off his flatbed, I knew. Your type telegraphs intent, a hubris of the highest order. But forget about him. He's consumed by his studies in Tabernacle. Let's talk about *you*."

Hagstrom tried not to whine or beg, but that seemed to be exactly what he was about to do. His vocal cords constricted and his voice raised nearly a fifth in pitch. "Please, mister, just cut me loose—"

"Oh, you'll be cut."

"—and you'll never ever see me again. I'll leave L.A., I'll leave California, I'll go all the way back to Syosset. I promise. Please, please don't take this any further."

"The Medusa Cult's breeding program gains momentum in the Southwest, and you Witches of the Left Hand recruit the breeders. I watched you woo her with your stage play romance, flowers, and false chivalry. All a neat little deception, eager to infest her birthwater with whatever parasite your masters favor. Wednesday, the day before yesterday, I saw you hand her a small bottle, and she smiled and stuffed it in her purse. You gave her potions and elixirs. Once they do their work, the innocent life inside her will mutate, sprout corruptions of flesh and spirit—and *her* needs, *her* priorities as a mother, will change. In the middle of the night, she will awaken ravenous to read forbidden books written by madmen in league with dark forces. *Those Others.*"

Hagstrom shook his head. The sound of the rustling plastic was maddening, the fetid air worse. The man's ramblings were utter nonsense, a delusion born of misfiring neurons, perhaps stoked by an obsession with a shadowy occult underground. But the word *amputation* stayed in his frontal lobe like it had been branded there.

"Are you talking about *Diedre*?" Hagstrom finally said. If he hadn't had that fourth Manhattan, if he had just backed off on the Vicodin, he may have been able to come out of that parking lot sucker punch all right, counter it with a jab to the solar plexus and an elbow across the nose. But he'd been loaded; booze and pills kept him not only pleasantly sloppy, but kept old trauma at bay. Before the whack on the skull from this crazy bastard, Hagstrom's only goal was to go home and sleep until noon. Now he was tasked with finding a way out of the restraints (an overwhelming problem with opioid-laden blood) and whatever needed to be done to get the purple paisley fuck out of here. He was in no position to enact violence on his captor, and Hagstrom knew he'd better start talking. At least it would buy him time to think.

"She's been a customer for three years. She and her husband live in a condo less than a quarter-mile away. I dog-sit for them when they travel. For God's sake, the bottle I gave her was *dog meds* I'd slipped into my laptop bag by mistake—*last winter*—when they went skiing in Big Bear. Diedre's positively thrilled to be pregnant. She bakes cookies at Christmas. *There's nothing wrong with her.*"

"Not until your influence. I watched for seven days." *Seven is secretive. Hidden agendas and goals.*

1+6 = 7.

16.

Gideon cut Flamingo Man's collar of duct tape and peeled away the crackling folds of the tarp. Shining with sweat like Lester Cornwall, the prisoner gulped fresh air.

"Look at me."

Hagstrom finally got a look at his captor. The man's face was slender but not gaunt, eroded with deep lines yet far from weather-beaten. Gray hair, cropped short, almost a Caesar cut. Bulging, hazel eyes beneath bushy, silver brows. He wore a janitor's coveralls with a faded Dickies logo on the breast. His right hand was gloved, but his left arm terminated in the ghastliest amputation stump Hagstrom had ever laid eyes upon. Bone and scar tissue formed a moonscape snarl of blunted nerves and yellowed, calloused skin. It looked as if he'd been attacked by a shark—or Josef Mengele.

"Behold, my war wound," Gideon said. "Born maimed and untainted. Unable to be swayed by the sinister left."

In 2007, during The Surge, the enormous offensive operation in Iraq, Lawrence Hagstrom had been a Navy Corpsman aboard the hospital ship USNS *Mercy*. He'd seen his share of mutilated men; he knew savagery's fingerprint. And now, in his late fifties, balding and rodent-faced, after years of trying to distance himself from such horrors, running as briskly as possible in the other direction, even as far as operating a flower stand in a bohemian art district, war had found him. Rye whiskey and Big Pharma formed an eager alliance to blot out memories of tile floors slick with blood and the screams of men missing half their meat, but tonight their alliance crumbled, and an enemy had breached the gate.

Hagstrom shook his head. Sweat stung his eyes. If he didn't straighten up and get a handle on his emotions, get his salesman charm in gear, he knew a similar barbarism would be upon him sooner than expected. Blood in the desert all over again.

"That's an *injury*," Hagstrom said, sniffing back a wad of snot and swallowing it.

Gideon's eyes narrowed. A neck artery throbbed. "No, Flamingo Man. It is a *gift*."

"I mean, you weren't *born* like that. Limb...deficiencies...don't scar, they're, well...smooth. It's not a *deformity*—that's a botched amputation."

A smoky corner of Gideon's mind opened, and through the rabbit warren of rooms and recollections, Mother's ghost records prowled. Jo Stafford crooned, *You Belong To Me.*

See the pyramids along the Nile...

On the yellowing kitchen tile, Father laid out an array of knives like an arms dealer setting up shop. He was shirtless, revealing a chest rife with scars, like those lines in the Andes people thought had been furrowed into the ground by ancient aliens. *Nascar?* No. *Nasca?* Yes. *Nasca. Father's chest looked like the Nasca Lines.*

It was early 1980, and Gideon still had a lot of growing up to do before his appointment with Lester Cornwall. The family lived in Danielsburg, the largest town in Walpurgis County, the one that offered the most awe-inspiring view of Walpurgis Peak, that horrendous granite fang that seemed to be everywhere you looked, regardless of direction. But the view wasn't awe-inspiring, it was dreadful. The mountain brooded over the county like a feudal lord, demanding supplication, fealty. To look upon it was to feel insignificant, gouged in the soul. It was the dark nexus of the permanent haunting of Walpurgis County, and wind sheared down its razor hide like a horse-drawn hearse.

And tonight, as the music ached and Father examined his blades, the wind curled beneath the eaves of their small house, moaning to be let in.

"Separation is Purification," Father said, cigarette bobbing. Heavy smoke choked the kitchen, hovering in the stove's jaundiced light. He was in his late thirties then, hair full and swept back from his clean brow, face lean and determined, physique taught and contoured by muscle and sinew. "Only then will you be able to complete my Mission."

"It's not a deformity," Mother cooed. Sitting on the kitchen counter, legs dangling, Gideon turned to her voice. Mother placed one hand between his shoulder blades, the other to the small of his back. "It is your war wound, decreed by birth. Father and I will show you how to use it and what it means. Our family has a Mission, and it is the Sinistra."

From the living room, where the wind's deep breath agonized the windows, a ghost recording sang, *Watch the sunrise on a tropic isle...*

This memory, clawing to the surface like mold breaching cracked paint, and the impudence of Flamingo Man to somehow suggest Gideon's blessed stump was something other than a shield of innocence and a harbinger of victory, twisted Gideon's features into a hag's ire.

"You know *nothing*," Gideon snapped.

(Later that night, Father headed to the Vanderbaum House, the House on Beltane Road. He took his knives...)

Gideon launched toward Hagstrom and grabbed handfuls of tarpaulin. He sprang upward like a bodybuilder executing a deadlift, pulling Hagstrom with him. Flamingo Man teetered; standing with his knees and ankles taped was nearly impossible.

Hagstrom wished he'd kept his mouth shut about that goddamn stump. He'd kicked the hornet's nest at the worst possible time, as the fantasy which fueled his captor's delusions was formidable. He was dragged across the plywood floor with little more than a series of small grunts. Now that Hagstrom could see, he looked at the space to assess his escape options.

Definitely, inside of a cargo container, the man hadn't lied. Bare incandescent bulbs in metal cages. Shelves full of bungee cords, duct tape, nails, hammers, and plastic wrap in sizes sold at restaurant supply stores. A pair of large metal cabinets, the kind he'd seen in workshops, used to store flammable or hazardous materials, stood on the far wall, doors closed. An ancient oscillating fan was mounted above, a relic from some black and white detective movie. A workbench with an old turntable had been wedged between the cabinets, the turntable plugged into a stereo receiver from the old days, and wires undoubtedly leading to the humming speakers he'd heard earlier. Below that, a five-gallon Home Depot bucket with the word *Pisspot* scrawled across it in Sharpie. The metal ladder he'd tumbled down was to his right now, beneath a hatch that led to fresh air—and anywhere but here.

Gideon angrily pushed Hagstrom into the wooden post. Bound and without balance, the back of Hagstrom's head struck the wooden beam with an oily *thunk*, and down he went.

Now Flamingo Man appeared exactly as Gideon imagined: a struggling pupa in a cocoon, a glistening larva on the verge of rebirth. Once the sinister hand was removed, the metamorphosis to disciple would take place, and he'd inhabit Tabernacle with the rest of them.

The recurring images in Gideon's mind fogged his focus, whispering distractions into the hollows of his skull as he went to his shelves and retrieved several bungee cords.

(There was a filleting knife, a chef's knife, a cleaver, one of those large, curved hunting knives)

(That's an injury...)

Something in the part of Gideon's mind that was still connected to physical reality—the buried container and his prisoner—made repeated attempts at raising a shield against encroaching memory. Every kill, even the pot-bellied, cashier-leering mailman, had been less effort.

(Father moved his hand over the resting blades like a stage magician. He looked past me, and I knew he and Mother were having a silent conversation.)

"Just look at me, Giddy," Mother said as she swept his hair from his forehead. Her bottom lip trembled, and Gideon smelled nervous sweat mixed with the sweet chemical tang of her Secret brand antiperspirant. Her eyelids moved so fast he was reminded of hummingbird wings. "Never take your eyes off me. Listen to Jo sing. She has such a beautiful voice."

Just remember darling, all the while...

"We all have a job to do, son," Father said. Usually, Father spoke with full, resonant authority—but now his voice was thick with dread. "I've hunted the Medusa Cult for decades, and tonight the Vanderbaum house *crawls* with them. After I clear the path, a new, purified *you* will keep it clean. Valor shall be your armor, and it will shine bright as the sun."

As the wind lowed like a wounded steer, Gideon looked at his father with wide, adoring eyes. A hero, a man on his Mission to save the world.

(Deformities do not scar...)

"Remember everything I taught you, Gideon. The numbers. The code."

Father set his huge palm over the back of Gideon's hand, pinning it to the kitchen counter. The blade scraped the tile when he grabbed the cleaver.

(That's a botched...)

Gideon whipped his neck around to Mother. Tears welled in the troughs of her eyes.

From the music, Gideon thought. *The sad music makes her cry.*

"Stay still."

(...amputation.)

Hagstrom watched as the man in coveralls stumbled backward, eyes on the mangled bulb where his left hand had been. Mouth bubbling with spit-choked words, he bumped into the workbench. Hanging saws rattled, and the turntable was nudged out of its coma with an audible scratch. In a shipping container ten feet below the desert, an old love song called from a world that no longer existed.

See the marketplace in old Algiers...

Gideon stomped to the rusted metal cabinets and yanked them open. Ugly fluorescent lights snapped on, illuminating the cabinets' interior. A fan-driven deathstink poured into the room. Hagstrom, who thought he'd seen it all, gagged. His four Manhattans came up like the last sputterings of a garden hose.

Captured Sinistra, the mummified disciples of Tabernacle, glared at Gideon and Hagstrom, frozen in their moment of gutless denial.

Send me photographs and souvenirs...

Some had been saddle stitched, forever matched as dreadful twins; faces merged at the cheek, perched atop two left hands mimicking a tarantula. Others gawked, sockets void and sightless, chins cupped in their palms like poets summoning trivialities. Teeth like miniature piano keys jammed into clay peered out from lips long crumbled away. Hair hung from some of them in frayed ropes; others were bald and resembled dried human fruit. Tongues reduced to dust formed a slope of talus pouring from long-silent mouths. Witches preserved, the recruiters recruited—to Tabernacle.

(Mother sobbing. I flinched at the last moment)
Stay Still.

"To prevent me from *becoming* one of them," Gideon whispered to his thirty-plus disciples.

Filthy, desiccated faces looked back at him. The endless sermons he'd given on the evils they'd perpetrated. How the desert had sated its greed for blood beneath his feet. With their final pleas ignored and long gone, they had very little say on the matter. He turned and faced the Flamingo Man.

(I screamed. Blood all over Father's face. Mother's hands like claws.)
Stay Still.

"I am bound by blood, Flamingo Man."

(I watched it twitch on the tile, half-separated. Father moaned. He said he was so, so sorry, but he grabbed the saw anyway.)

The wind, that fossil hearse on a downhill collision course with a young boy named Gideon, brayed its warning to all reaches of the globe: *Duhruuuh.*

Hagstrom was short on options. The restraints were inescapable, the cabinet's horrors a preview of hell. He'd triggered an awakening, and there was little doubt about how it would play out. War hits home, and everybody bleeds.

"Separation *is* Purification," Gideon said, a child to

whom the solution to a difficult problem has just become evident. "Now I understand. Now I know."

Just remember when a dream appears...

Turning to Flamingo Man, whose eyes had become boiled eggs set into his slender rat face, Gideon offered only a wide lupine grin before he whispered, "Now *you'll* know."

Gideon reached for the saw. Not long now until Flamingo Man revealed his true intentions and surrendered the names of Sinistra and their Medusa Cult handlers.

Hand over his heart, Father's Man of Valor swayed to the music.

I remember. Father took his knives with him but left the cleaver in the sink so their blood could not possibly mix with mine.

Jo Stafford's smoky timbre, the sound of Mother's war sacrifice, filled Tabernacle.

You belong to me...

Southpaw

49

50

~Kyle Toucher~

KYLE TOUCHER (rhymes with voucher) wrote his first Godzilla story in grade school, read *The Exorcist* at the age of fourteen, then bought a guitar when *Black Sabbath: Volume 4* changed his life. Through his twenties, he fronted the influential Nardcore crossover band Dr. Know, made records, and hit the road. Later, he moved into the Visual Effects field, he bagged eight Emmy nominations and two awards for *Firefly* and *Battlestar: Galactica*. Recent film credits include *Top Gun: Maverick* and *Devotion*.

He lives with a lovely woman, five cats, two dogs, and several guitars in a secure, undisclosed location, where a new novel is underway.

His debut novel, *Live Wire*, was published in April 2023 from Crystal Lake Publishing: getbook.at/Live_Wire.

Life Returns, his Gothic horror novella based on the classic Dr. Know song of the same name, was released for free on the Kindle format in March 2023: getbook.at/LifeReturns.

Bibliography

BILLY BEAUCHAMP, DISCOUNT EXORCIST, Culture Cult Press, 2022

DECEMBER 21, 1984 Crystal Lake Publishing, 2022

FLIGHT 2320, Crystal Lake Publishing, 2022

FLIGHT 2320: WIRE WITCH Crystal Lake Publishing, 2023

FREEZER BURN, Crystal Lake Publishing, 2022

HELL'S INFIRMARY, Teleport Magazine, 2021

LIFE RETURNS Crystal Lake Publishing, 2023

LIVE WIRE Crystal Lake Publishing, 2023

NOTE TO SANDERSON, Crystal Lake Publishing, 2022

STRANGE ACRES, DBND Publishing, 2021

THE HOUSE ON BELTANE ROAD, Black Hare Press, 2022

THE NIGHTMAN'S LAST SHIFT, Crystal Lake Publishing, 2022

THE RED EYE TO SALEM, Crystal Lake Publishing, 2022

THIS IS A GREEDY, JEALOUS HOUSE, Crystal Lake

Publishing, 2022

WE SHOULD BE ON OUR WAY FROM HERE, Crystal Lake Publishing, 2022

WITCHFYNDRE, Crystal Lake Publishing, 2022

Connect

Website: www.kyletoucher.monster

Twitter: @kyletoucher

54

Black Hare Press

55

BLACK HARE PRESS is a small, independent publisher based in Melbourne, Australia. Founded in 2018, our aim has always been to champion emerging authors from all around the globe and offer opportunities for them to participate in speculative fiction and horror short story anthologies.

Connect: linktr.ee/blackharepress

56

Invited

Coming Soon from Black Hare Press

Invited

by Nicole Little

*R*ock a bye baby…"
The eerie refrain followed Alex up the stairs as he ran as fast as his little legs could carry him…away from his mother.

She scraped the blade of the knife along the wood panelling; a trail of bloody footprints came behind her, droplets spattered in a macabre pattern across her summer dress.

"On the treetop…"

Alex dropped to all floors and crawled through the darkness along the hall, struggling to control his frantic breathing. On his eighth birthday, nearly a year ago, his dad had given him a Swiss army knife. If he could get to his room, if he could reach between the mattress and grab it—he might have a chance.

"When the wind blows…"

He knew Birdie and Bea were dead. He'd seen their bodies in the dining room, still sitting at the table where they'd been eating breakfast. She'd slit their throats. Two-year-old Andy was being unusually quiet for such a normally noisy toddler. Alex hoped it meant he was napping and not the alternative—that she had gotten to him first, before Alex came home from school.

"The cradle will rock..."

A small giggle spluttered from his mothers' mouth as she tiptoed down the hallway. With a sinking feeling in his stomach Alex realized he wasn't going to make it to his room, the last at the end of the row, it was too far. Taking a deep breath, he jumped up and sprinted with all he had, sliding his way into his parent's room, tumbling into the walk-in closet and slamming the door shut.

"When the bow breaks..."

He knew she was in the room, could hear her voice as she sung the lullaby. Frantic he felt along the wall for the light switch. The small room burst to life and Alex found himself surrounded by the heady scent of his mothers' perfume, her clothing and shoes, fur coats and leather jackets, hats, and purses…and his dad's old baseball bat.

"The cradle will fall..."

He grabbed it, felt the heft of it in his hand. It was solid wood.

"And down will come Alex..."

Three years of softball meant he had perfected his swing. He'd need a home run to get out of this one.

"Cradle and all..."

She rapped on the door with her knuckles: once, twice,

three times. "I know there's no lock in there you naughty boy, and there is no where else to hide. Come on out now and give mommy a hug." She jiggled the doorknob and Alex knew it was now or never.

"Ok mommy. I'm coming out."

"Good boy. Always my good boy."

Alex threw open the door and rushed at her, smashing the head of the bat into her stomach. Her breath exploded in a *whoosh*, but he didn't stop pushing at her until she came up against the bedroom wall; the knife in her hand clattered to the floor. Alex bent to pick it up; he felt the slam of his mothers' fist at the side of his head and black spots danced in front of his eyes. She slapped him across the face again and the sharp tang of blood flooded his mouth.

Annabella Desrosiers deftly snatched up the knife from where it had fallen, her breathing rough and shallow. "Naughty boy. Very naughty boy. Like your sisters and brother. It's time for you to learn your lesson."

She had several inches and about sixty pounds on him, but Alex had the bat. And he didn't hesitate. He swung with all his might. The solid wood connected with her side, just beneath her elbow. He was positive he heard a rib crack, maybe two. She screamed, her breathing grew even more ragged, and spittle flew from her lips. Before she had a chance to react, Alex swung the bat again, this time aiming for her face. The bat hit her temple with a sickening crunch. She folded to the floor, writhing and moaning, as blood ran from her nose and ears. She raised a hand towards Alex but all he could see were the images of his dead sisters burned into his memory. He hit her again, smashing at the hand, her fingers bending backwards with a sharp snap. She screamed and he hit her again.

And again.

And again.

Until the screams had long stopped and the rush of blood in his ears had calmed.

***

When they found him a few days later—when the kids hadn't show up for school and no one had answered the phone—he was sitting at the dining room table eating peanut butter with a spoon, explaining batting averages to his decomposing sisters.

www.ingramcontent.com/pod-product-compliance
Lightning Source LLC
Chambersburg PA
CBHW050747180726
48003CB00020B/2092